W9-BUB-867

SWIM TEAM

MTA
MetroCard
MAPS
DIRECTIONS
NEW YORK
FLORIDA
GOODBYE BREE!
from Ms. Jackson's Class
Gonna Miss You! Tasha
Adios Bree -Lucia
Pasta la Pizza, baby -Joey
Florida Pocket Wildlife Guide
LEATHERBACK SEA TURTLE
BOTTLENOSE DOLPHIN
AMERICAN ALLIGATOR

JOHNNIE CHRISTMAS

SWIM TEAM

HARPER alley
An Imprint of HarperCollins*Publishers*

For future swimmers,
wherever they may be

1

Butterflies

Brooklyn
Alligators?!
Yep.
And sea turtles?
Yep. They got those in Florida, too.

How big is the new tub, Dad?
We're NOT getting a manatee, Bree.

But I did get that puzzle you wanted for the trip!
>Gasp<
Daaad!

It's very advanced. We can get a simpler—
No WAY, Dad! I'm gonna solve it!

All right, then! Let's hit the road!

I'll figure it out in no time.
Too bad when I do I won't be able to show my friends...
...since I'll be at a different school in a different state...
Hi, I'm Bree.
Y'know...

You going to this new school reminds me of the butterfly effect.
What's that?

I never told you about the butterfly effect?
No...
And this is my dad, Ralph.

Dad got into a training program in Florida. IT or coding I think.
Plus a job as a delivery driver. So really, he'll have two jobs.
That's why we're moving.
It's a PROCESS that explains how little changes can have a BIG effect... It goes like this...
A butterfly flaps its wings far away, let's say, over Beijing.

Can it be Brooklyn?
Sure. A butterfly flaps its wings over BROOKLYN.

New Jersey
The flapping makes a small change to the WIND...

PROUD PARENT OF AN HONOR ROLL STUDENT
South Carolina
Which makes another small change to the waves.

All those little changes add up to BIG changes...

Florida

...and by the time those changes appear far, far away...
HOLYOKE PREP SWIM TEAM!
5-TIME CHAMPIONS!
Like Florida?
Sure. Like Florida.
Welcome to PALMETTO SHORES
Those tiny wings can lead to whipping winds, churning seas, and a mighty STORM...

Or a perfectly sunny day. You never know! Small changes. Big unpredictable effects!
DINER

It happens with people, not just butterflies!
We affect other people in ways we can't guess.
Like a puzzle I don't know the solution to yet?
Exactly!

You'll have an effect on your new school, too! Maybe as part of the math club?!
School is very important to Dad.

He always says...
Remember, an education is one thing no one can take away from you.
Focus on your books. Worry about making friends later.

Holyoke is going all the way to State this year!
AGAIN!
Their coach is a bit INTENSE, no?

That's what it takes to WIN!
If you say so.

Lots of swimming and water puns on the menu.
Well, look at that...

MENU
Ice Cream Float
Mussel Bowls
Sea Biscuits
Bermuda Pie Angles
Orca Julius
Boatload O' Fries
Oceanside Omelet
Steamboat Baske
Pearly Bird Spec
Breamsicle
Beach Stack
Surfin' Tur

I guess the owner likes swimming?

More juice, dear?

Maybe just a "splash," ma'am.

Get it, Dad?
Very "punny," Bree.

BREE'S FAVORITE THINGS

STUFF BREE DOESN'T LIKE!

SPORTS!

POOLS!

NOT HAVING FRIENDS ANYMORE!

YOU'LL NEVER MAKE NEW FRIENDS. EVEEER-RRR!
Bree!
Huh?!

This is it!
Our new home!

Let's get moved in!

Excited?!

POOL RULES
Icky pool.

Do I get to pick my room?!
Pick ANY room you want!

As long as it's the **small** one.
Heh heh.
Very funny, Dad.

Almost done! You okay with that box? Looks a little heavy.
I've got it!

Great! I've got something for the landlord.
Actually it's heavier than I—

Be right back!
DAAAD!

What did he pack in this box?
BRICKS?!

WELCOME!
You must be Bree!!
GAAH!

Yes... Yes, I am—
I'm Etta, I live upstairs. I just met your dad!
He tells me you like puzzles?

My arms are getting—
I love puzzles!
Jigsaw puzzles mostly.
I get puzzles made from my old photos.
MAIL

Puzzles of my cat, or vacations, or old friends!

Looks like she could use a rescue...

We can work on a puzzle **together**!
Oh. Okay.

Hi,
Ms. Etta.
Clara!
On your way to
the pool?

You
know it.
Let me
know if—
See you
LATER,
Ms. Etta!

She'll talk
your ear off if
you let her.
Ha ha,
she's not
so bad.

I'm Bree!
Clara!
SHAKE

We probably go to the same school.
Eniith? Eniiith?
Yep, Enith Brigitha Middle!

Maybe I'll see you there!
Okay! See ya!

Bree, there you are! Is that the box with the books?

No wonder it's so heavy!

Been looking all over for this. HEE HEE.
DAAAD! C'mon!

First day of school
6:59

ACK-
CLICK!
7:00

SO EXCITED!

Now let's see...which folder shall I pick...
My **FAVORITE** folder, of course!
TAP TAP TAP

Bree. Sit down and finish your breakfast.
Too excited! First day of school!
JUMP JUMP

Enith Brigitha Middle School
ASK QUESTIONS! STAY CURIOUS!
ENITH BRIGITHA MIDDLE SCHOOL

Now, where is the office?

BREE?!

I thought that was you!
Clara!

Looking for the office?
I can't find it.

I'll take you. But first let me show you around the school!
Yes, please!

Our school's not fancy. We don't have the newest stuff.
But it's really chill. You'll fit right in!

There's my friend Humberto. He's an artiste.
See? Chill!

WELCOME 2 MATH CLUB
Oh, there's the math club!

Math's my favorite subject. What about you?
LUNCH!
Just kidding. Probably swim class.

I'm trying out for the swim team this year. I wish I were better at math, though.

I can help with math! We can be study buddies!
BET!

Well, there's the office. I'll see ya later!
WELCOME STUDENTS!
See ya, Clara!

Moments later
And for your fourth-period elective?
Math Puzzles, please.

Unfortunately Math Puzzles is **FULL.**

Full?! But...
...it's the only elective I wanna take.

Sorry.

Okay, how about Yearbook?
Lemme check...

Sorry, that's full, too.

Origami Round Table?

Full.

Bookkeepers Corner?
Full.

Swamplands Study Group?
Full.

Sewer Maintenance Seminar?
...Sounds stinky...
Full.

Wait. Here's one!
Yes?!

Swim 101.
Swim 101?!

Fourth period

Welcome to Swim 101.

I'm Coach Pinella.
Before we start...
Is there anyone here who can't swim?

I...

Uhm...

Uh.
Speak up. Anyone?
No one?

Good.

Before we start class, a little history...
Did you know our school is named after the first Black woman to win an olympic swimming medal?
And our swim team almost won the State Championship!
A long time ago. But still...

So try out for the swim team.
It might be your last chance. The school district wants to sell the land our pool is on to Smoothie Palace.
But maybe they won't if we win a few swim meets. You can make a difference!

But, I like smoothies, Coach.
What flavors will they have?

45 minutes later
Okay. See you all here tomorrow.
Don't forget your swimsuits!

Bree? I'm Humberto. You're Clara's friend, right?

You looked pretty nervous in class.
Maybe a little.

Don't worry. Everyone passes Swim 101.

Unless you drown!
WHY DON'T YOU KNOW HOW TO SWIM?
IT MUST BE YOUR FAULT!

Back at home
Puzzle. Down.
And help set the table, please.

Caribbean flavors!
Beans.
Plantains.
Rice.

So! Tell me all about your first day! How was Math Puzzles?

MATH BOWL
FIRST PLACE
BREE HANLEY
1

I can't wait for you to bring another math award home!

Math Puzzles was full.
What?!

That's an outrage!
I KNOW!
I ended up in Swim 101 instead.

Oh!

Well, that's not so bad.
It's NOT bad... It's TERRIBLE!
Swimming is an important skill, too.

Geez, Dad, whose side are you on?!
You'll get Math Puzzles NEXT semester.

I hope so.
Now. Please pass the plantains.

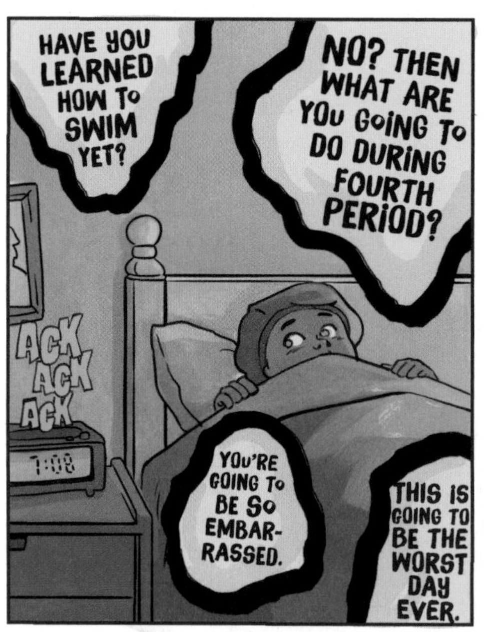
HAVE YOU LEARNED HOW TO SWIM YET?
NO? THEN WHAT ARE YOU GOING TO DO DURING FOURTH PERIOD?
ACK ACK ACK
7:08
YOU'RE GOING TO BE SO EMBARRASSED.
THIS IS GOING TO BE THE WORST DAY EVER.

NO!
Today is going to be a great day!

At school
HOME OF THE
MIGHTY MANATEES

So awesome that we have social studies together.
Hello, fellow Manatees!

Bree, we'll be late for swim class if we don't hurry!

You coming?
>GULP<

YOU'RE DOOMED.
EXIT

See you at the pool!
Okay.
WOMEN

DID YOU FORGET YOUR LOCK?
DID YOU FORGET YOUR SWIM-SUIT?

MAYBE YOU SHOULD HIDE IN THE LOCKER ROOM.
LOCKER ROOM
DON'T GO OUT THERE!

DON'T GO OUT THERE!

Hey! Hey! No splashing!

TOO DEEP.
SO DOOMED.
Sorry, Coach!
Busted!

THEY'RE ALL LOOKING AT YOU.
SCARED. SO SCARED.
THEY ALL LOOK SO COMFORTABLE IN THE WATER.
CAN'T DO IT.
EVERYONE'S WONDERING WHY YOU'RE NOT IN A SWIMSUIT.
REAL DEEP POOL.

Coach, I...
Yeah?
WHAT WILL COACH SAY?
NO GOOD.

...I...I feel sick.
You know where the nurse's office is?

See you here tomorrow.
Okay.
WHAT ARE YOU GOING TO DO TOMORROW?!
YOU CAN'T BE "SICK" EVERY DAY.

WHY DID WE MOVE TO FLORIDA OF ALL PLACES?
POOLS AND BEACHES EVERYWHERE.
EV
Grrr...
NO WAY I'LL EVER BE—
YOU'LL SPEND YOUR WHOLE LIFE COMING UP WITH EXCUSES TO AVOID THE WATER.

CAN'T—
CAN'T DO IT.
MIGHT AS WELL START MAKING A LIST NOW.
POP
I...
FEEL SICK.

SCHOOL NURSE

I don't feel so bad anymore.

What to do for the rest of the period...?

LIBRARY

WORLD OF
I'll get ahead on my other school assignments!

2

Making Waves

The first thing you do when moving to a new town...
BANK

...is all the boooring stuff.
...options to fit your needs...
BOSS

How's your daughter adjusting?
This is such a wonderful neighborhood.

I made some of my BEST friends when I was her age!
CLICK CLICK CLICK

DENTIST

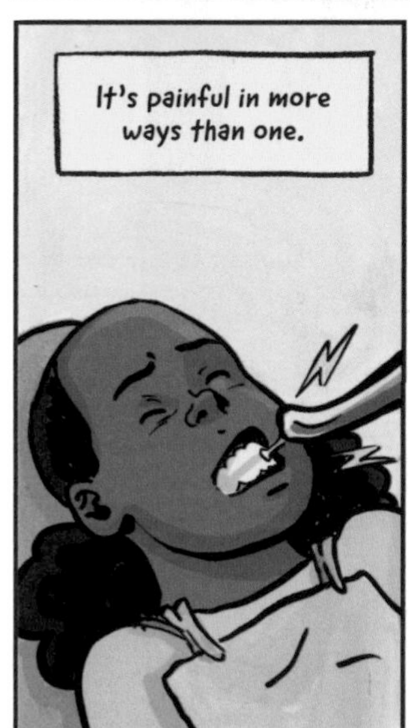
It's painful in more ways than one.

MANATEES
Hang on. We're almost done!
Dw'I'm Dw'hanging Dw'on...

How you doing, kiddo?
My teeth feel sand-blasted.
See you in four months!

AFTER your homework, you can have park time with your friends.

Smells like Ms. Etta's making dinner!
Mmmmm!

Ms. Etta's cat is named Cornelius!
Hi, Cornelius!
Welcome

Thanks for looking after her, Etta!
My pleasure! Come on in, Bree!

Make yourself at home!

Is this one of your jigsaw puzzles?
Yes! Do you like it?

It's great!

Z Z Z Z
GLUE

And here's dinner.
This looks delicious, Ms. Etta!

African American delights!
Black-eyed peas.
Collards.
Corn bread.

The collards were my grandmother's recipe.
Slow cooked, so take your time and really enjoy the flavors!
I will!
Oh, your dad said you should finish dinner and homework before the park.

BEFORE?!

Both homework AND dinner?!
4:45

But my friends will be here soon!

Now, for the BLACK-EYED PEAS, I like to add a dash of—
Good gracious!
CHOMP CHOMP

Soon

DONE!

BreEEEEeee!

Clara?!
Down here!

We're going to the park.

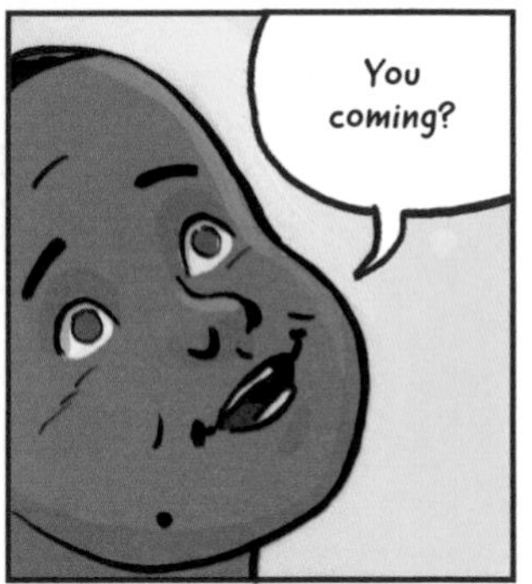
You coming?

So you design costumes for the school plays?
Yes!

I'm head costume designer of the drama club.

I was even written about in the **SCHOOL PAPER**!
Wow!

Our new play is called *Class of Their Own*. A drama about kids in a wealthy school—
Sounds like you're describing Holyoke Prep.

What's Holyoke Prep?

A private school in town.
A school of rich snobs!
Holyoke... more like "Holy Yuck"!

Clara's upset because Holyoke wins the State Championship every year.

We almost won. Once...
ALMOST. And that was, like, *fifty* years ago.

Yeah, well, we're gonna whup 'em this year!

I'll believe it when I see it, Clara.

Whoa...

Who's that?

Speak of the devil... That's Tinsley.
Oh...

Cool!

We'll make it to State, and we're going to win the RELAY MEDLEY.
Well, good luck! Tinsley is a swimming powerhouse.
Um, Clara...

I'm not scared of Holyoke. Or Tinsley!
They win a few races, and people act like they walk on water.

"A few races"?
?
...Behind you!

*Not-name-brand shoes

And you think YOU'RE going to make it to STATE?
What do our clothes or my iPod have to do with going to State?

Has your school ever won a championship?
We almost—

Know what we call people who "almost" win championships?

LOSERS!
Whatever, Keisha!

YOUR school shouldn't be named after a swimming champ.
OURS should.

flip!
And it will be someday. When you become a famous swimmer, Tinsley.

Someone woke up on the wrong side of the bed this morning.

What's YOUR story?
You trying out for the "team," too?
No, I wasn't planning on—

Of course not. You don't even LOOK like you can swim.
All right, Tinsley. We've had enough of your—

I mean, you CAN swim, can't you?

No way!
Are you SERIOUS?!

!
!

HA HA HA HA HA HA HA

Put THAT in your play, Humberto!

You're in the right company, new girl.
These losers barely know how to swim either.

We'll see YOU in the pool, Clara.

Is that why you've been missing swim class?
I want to go home now.

If you keep skipping, they'll send Haylie to find you.
She's the HALL MONITOR!!

She hunts kids who skip class.
See you guys in school tomorrow.

What was up with that?
It's true. Holyoke Prep dominates in swimming.

Most swimmers would love to be on their team 'cause they always win State.

The State Championship is a BIG swim meet held every year.
I figured that part out.

Champions or not, Holyoke seems like a school full of jerks.
Tell that to my mom. She keeps trying to get me into Holyoke!

Joke's on her.
I'll never pass the math part of the entrance exam!

Oh! I forgot to give you this!

I made it in art class.
It's a friendship bracelet.

I don't care if you can't swim.

You're my friend.

Let's get back home!

The next day
Good luck in swim class today, Bree!
Th-thanks...

HUMBERTO PROBABLY TOLD EVERYONE YOU CAN'T SWIM!

THEY'LL ALL STARE AT YOU.

I don't feel good. Maybe I'll go see the nurse again...
YOU'LL BE SO EMBARRASSED.
THEY'RE GONNA LAUGH AT YOU, TOO.

Where's your hall pass?
HALL MONITOR
WELL?!

Oh no! Haylie the Hall Monitor!

No one skips class on **MY WATCH!**
ZOOOOM

Maybe I'll hide in the cafeteria?

Uh-oh!
ZOOOM

ZOOOM
Any skippers in here?!

Oh no! Dead end!

No one gets away from...

...me!

Where's your—
MUSIC CLUB

RRRINNGG
MUSIC CLUB

TOD
Hmmm...
HALL MONITOR

Hi, Dad.
I'm...

...home.
You've been skipping class?!

What's going on, Bree?
You LOVE school!
I—

Are you being BULLIED?
No, Dad.

Then what is it?
My ONLY CHILD is a JUVENILE DELINQUENT!!!

I'm scared of the pool.
I don't know how to swim.

Oh, okay. We can work on that.
IT'S TOO LATE FOR YOU TO LEARN.
It's too late for me to learn.

Nonsense. You learned math.
And now it's your favorite subject.

In fact, your true talent isn't math. It's that you—
What?

You never give up.
Not on a hard math problem or a difficult puzzle.
Just apply that to **swimming.**

Now! We're going to find you some private swim lessons.

HOLYOKE
HOLYOKE
The lessons are at Holyoke Prep?
It's the only class available on such short notice.
Why?
No reason.

Here for the pool?

Head right in!
munch munch

Minutes later
Have fun!
So glad to have you, Bree!

It'll be fun. You'll see.
Wow, this place is huge.

Yeah, a lot of important swim meets are held here.

Oh, Bree, not that pool...

Huh?

...This pool!
CAUTION

Z
Z
Z

The *kiddie pool*?!!

This will be fine.
These kids seem nice.
Z
Z
Z
Z
Z

It's not like I know anyone here—

HAHAHAHAHAHA

Oh. My. God.
It's the "swimmer"!

Are you taking classes **FROM** the preschoolers?
Look! She can't even swim as good as them!

Aren't you **EMBARRASSED**?!
I would be!

Hey kid, take good care of her.

Don't you girls have somewhere else to be?

Bree? Bree?!

Over so soon?
Bree?

The next day
Uggggggghhhhhh
ACK
ACK
ACK
7:15

That's it!

Fourth-period bell
Maybe I can convince the administrator to switch me out of Swim 101.
Maybe she likes apples? Maybe if I cut her grass or...

No, that's wrong. I'll go into the library and come up with a better plan.

There she is.
HALL MONITOR

Where's your hall pass?

You won't get away **THIS** time!
HALL MONITOR

HALL MONITOR
Get back here!

Almost got you...!

Uh?!

SCREEEEECH!

You...you just left the BUILDING!
HALLMON
TRACK MEET TODAY AWAY

You've gone from skipping CLASS...

To skipping SCHOOL!
I...I...

TRACK MEET TODAY AWAY
ENITH BRIGITHA MIDDLE SCHOOL

Back home

What am I gonna do now?!

Go to my room and think?
AND MAYBE HIDE THERE UNTIL YOU'RE EIGHTY!

ZZZZZ
I wonder what Dad is going to say when he finds out...
BUMP
POOL
Oh NO!!
My math homework!

It'll be ruined!
Can this day get ANY worse?!
POOL RULES

?

WH...WHOA!
SLIP!

SPLASH!

H...H...

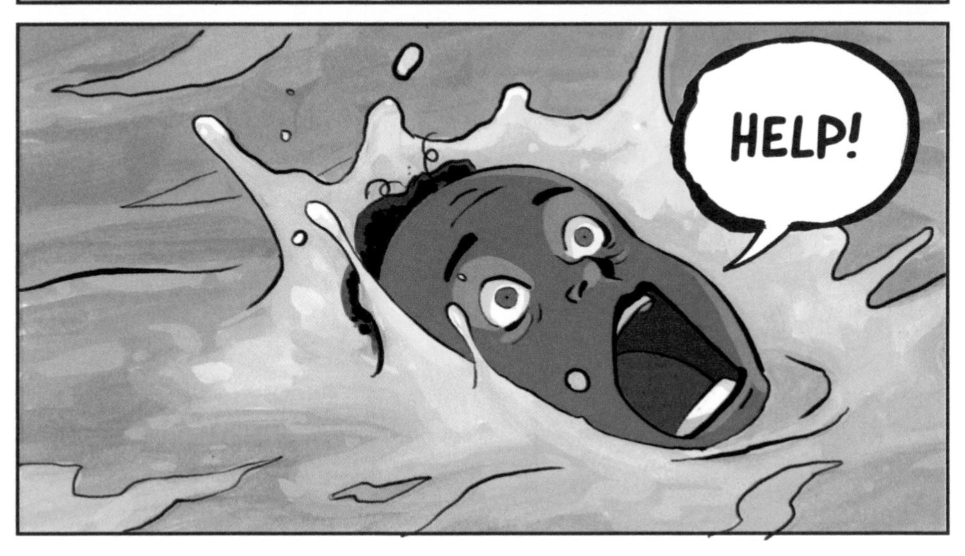
HELP!

BREE!!

HOLD ON, BREE!

I'M COMING!
HOP!

I'M COMING, BREE!
KICK.
KICK.

SPLASH!

>GASP<

I've got you!
HUFF! HUFF!

Are you okay?

Soon.
Etta's apartment
Thank you, Ms. Etta.
tweeeet!

Promise me you'll be more careful around the pool.

I will, Ms. Etta.
Your daddy should be here soon.

You spilled your puzzle.
Oh, don't bother with those.

I've got all weekend to put it back together.

I can help.

?

Ms. Etta, I didn't know you were a swimmer.
Oh yes, dear. A long time ago...All through school, in college, and even a few years professionally.

No way...
You swam at
my middle
school?
Yes!
That's where
it all started
for me.

The school had a
different name then, but
we almost won a
championship that year!

You were
on THAT
team?!
DING DONG
We were
pretty
good.
That
must be
your dad!

BREE!

Are you
all right?
It was
really scary.

Thanks for being there, Etta.

Let's get you home.
M... Ms. Etta...

Ms. Etta, can you teach me how to swim?

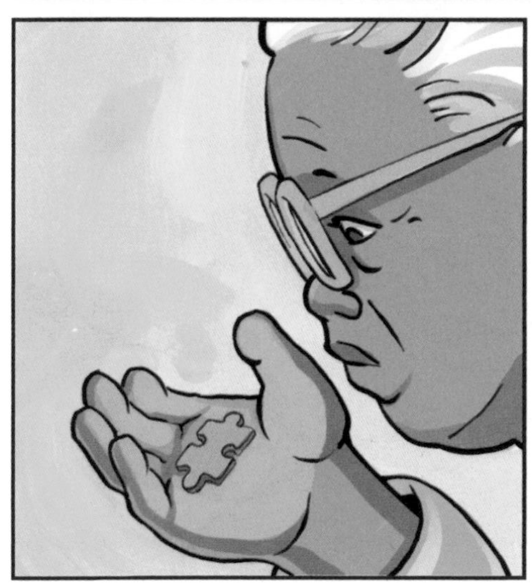

Ms. Etta's done enough. She's very busy.
Please?

I'll make you a nice papaya soup.

Bree.

We'll start first thing Saturday morning.

3

The Deep End

We bought some swim gear for today!
Your dad put a PRETTY BIG bag in the trunk.
How much swim gear?

THUMP
THUMP
THUMP
Nervous?

There's nothing to be nervous about.

It'll be fun. You'll see.

But... Black people aren't good at swimming.

I'm good at swimming, **AND** I'm Black.
So that can't be **TRUE.**

Matter of fact, Black people swim, fish, canoe, surf, and everything else you can think of.

You come from a long line of swimmers, all Black people do.
Me?
Yes.

Really?

Really.

From ancient Africa to modern Africa...
from Chicago to Peru...
in seas, rivers, lakes, and pools...

Black people have always swum and always will.
The art of swimming is handed down, generation after generation.
Then why can't so many of my friends swim?
Well... that's where it gets complicated...

WHITES ONLY
In America, laws were passed that limited Black people's access to beaches, lakes, and swimming pools.
Lack of access meant fewer Black people swimming. So fewer Black people passed it down.
Opposition to these conditions were often met with violence.
From the murder of Eugene Williams in Chicago, 1919...
to acid poured in a pool with protesters in St. Augustine, Florida, 1964.

So the knowledge was scattered. Like a jigsaw puzzle with missing pieces.
But, regardless, we kept fighting and, eventually, the laws were changed.
John Lewis, protesting a segregated pool in Cairo, Illinois, 1962.
Beach protests in Connecticut, 1975.
FREE THE BEACHES
David Isom, a teenager breaking the color line at a Florida pool in 1958.

Still, there were few, if any, pools in our neighborhoods. And they were often small or poorly maintained...
Making it hard to put our swimming culture back together...
Going to public pools in other neighborhoods often meant facing discrimination. It happened to me when I was a girl, and it still happens today.
Not knowing how to swim is **NOT** your fault, Bree.
Today we'll begin putting your piece into the puzzle.

HECKS
ASHED
WESTERN ONION
WO
FAMILY D
Here we are!
It's an old conservatory that's been turned into a pool!

Inside
ECEPTION
Welcome!
It's a magical place!
And the same pool I learned to swim in as a girl.
Got your swimsuit?
Oh, I'm prepared!
Okay! Get changed, and I'll see you poolside!

Moments later
I'm not taking ANY chances!
Oh dear... Bree.

We won't need some of these today.

C'mon in, Bree.
YOU ALMOST DROWNED LAST TIME.
IT'S DAN-GER-OUS.

It's safe. I promise.

Stay calm.
Stay calm.
Stay calm.

Soon
...Those were our pool safety rules. We'll go over them next time, too.

Our first lesson is simple. Hold your breath underwater for five seconds. Can you do that?
I think so...

Starting in 3...2...1...

1
2
3
4
5

>GAAAASP<

Good! Now try it floating facedown.

Very good!
Easy, right?

It's even easier on your back. Let's give that a try.
Okay!

THUMP THUMP THUMP

THUMP
THUMP
THUMP

THUMP
THUMP
THUMP

COUGH! COUGH!! COUGH!!!

It's okay.
It'll be okay.
Wanna try again?
N-no.
Okay. That's enough for today.
Remember, everyone learns step-by-step.
Learning a little more each time.

Adding more pieces.
It's a process.

You're already better than you were this morning, right?
Yes, ma'am.

And tomorrow you'll be better than today.
TOMORROW?!
But I have a sleepover at Clara's tonight!!

Then don't sleep in.
I'm picking you up **bright** and early.

The sleepover
Bree, you're here!

Bree, your hair!

Hi, Mrs. Carter. Hi, Clara.
I was in the pool for a while.
It's a mess of tangles.

I can deal with it tomorrow.
It'll be even MORE tangled tomorrow if you sleep on it like that.

I can fix—
Me and Bree can do it!

Uh, I don't think that's such a good idea...
Sure it is!

Soon
You need a hairstyle that's good for the pool. Let's see...

We'll detangle...

moisturize and section. And let's try a few styles!

Too...complicated?
Gotcha.

Regal! But maybe too much work to maintain?
On it.

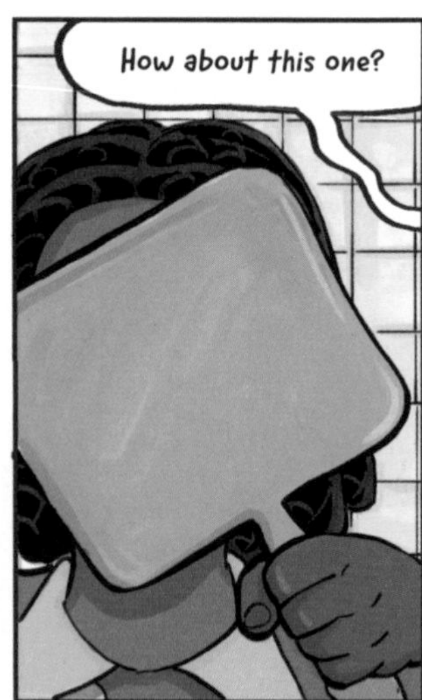
How about this one?

I love it!

Lookin' good, girls!
When Bree learns to swim, we can hang out at the pool, too.

Let's not get our hopes TOO high.
We're gonna be swim sisters, you'll see!
Let's watch some swimming videos.

I'll show you some good tips.

The next day
Let's try floating on your back again.

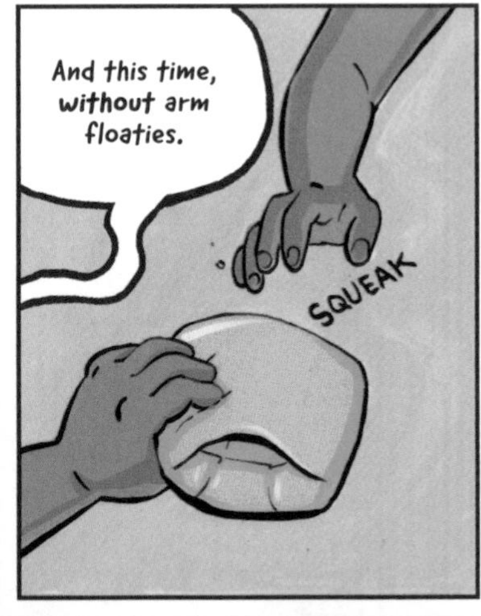
And this time, without arm floaties.
SQUEAK

GAH!
Let's try again.

Hold it. Holllllllld iiiiit!

Ms. Etta?
Lean into it.

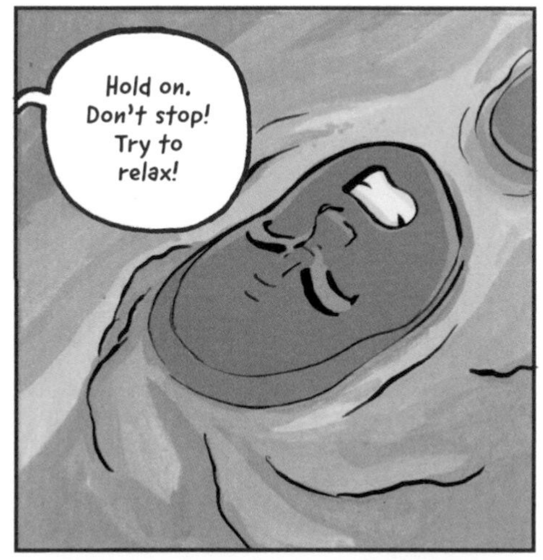
Hold on. Don't stop! Try to relax!

You're doing it, Bree. You're floating!

Now let's try a few strokes!
Just like with floating, we're going to break it down into little steps...

Days pass
Ms. Etta started taking me to the pool every day after school. It became our routine.

Don't be afraid to splash!

Puuuush!
Each day, she'd teach a new skill to add to what I'd already learned.
3FT
Like we do in math class or like when I'm working on my puzzle.

Resist the urge to pull your head backward, out of the water, to breathe.

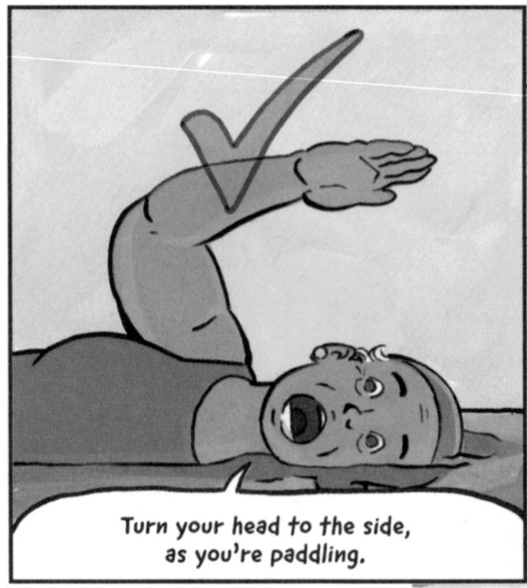
Turn your head to the side, as you're paddling.

Keep treading, Bree!
Okay! Oka—
Uh-oh!
Let's try it again.
The pool started to feel more and more familiar.
I got used to the feel of tile floors and the smell of chlorine.
I started to like the pool.

Weeks pass

Every day, everyone at the pool cheered me on.

I started to understand what Ms. Etta meant about how positive swimming culture is.

I started going back to Swim 101, but I was still shy about swimming around the kids at school.
No horsing around!

Dad continued to work all day and take training courses at night.

We saw less and less of each other.

Z
Z
Dad!

Big test tomorrow?
Huh?! Oh yeah. Real big.

Yeah... me too...

Seeing less of each other was our new routine.

Fantastic, Bree. You're getting the hang of it!

Now it's time to try treading in deep water.

The deep end of the pool
Ready?
6 FEET

I'll take the noodle, please.
It's all you.

>GASP<

You're in control. Don't be afraid...

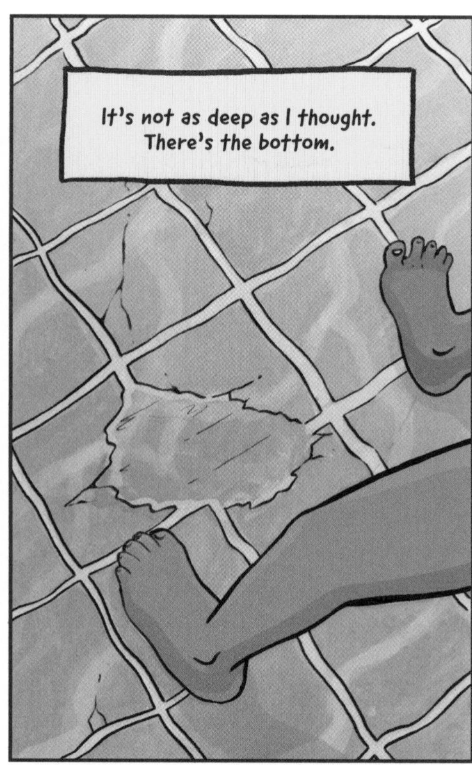
It's not as deep as I thought.
There's the bottom.

And there's Mr. O'Leary's
hairy chicken legs.

And my favorite
handrail.

The surface is only right above my head!
Just keep moving your arms and legs like Ms. Etta showed you.
It's working! I'm starting...
To rise.

>GASP<
You're doing it, Bree!

You're a swimmer now!

A little later
I'm going to miss swimming lessons with you.
But now you can take what I showed you...

...and have new adventures at the pool.
Like a new exciting puzzle!

Speaking of, did you find all the missing pieces from your spilled puzzle?

...From the day you saved me in the pool?
No, but I've got a new one to celebrate your new beginning!
1000 PIECE
JIGSAW PUZZLE

It's been an honor teaching you, Bree.

Puzzle making is so fun...
1000 PIECE JIGSAW PUZ

Puzzle making here I come!
FLOP!

4

Sink or Swim

A C?! My dad's gonna KILL me if I bring home a C!
That's the best I can do, Bree. You missed a lot of class.

SWIM TEAM TRYOUTS
Fakey McFakerson
Jaws Henry
Franny O'Fishstick

Fakey McFakerson?!
TEAM

Students, listen up.
The swim team tryout sheet has only three names on it.

And I'm pretty sure two of them are FAKE.

So, I'm gonna try something different. Phyllis, Jane, Toni, you're all good swimmers.
Get in the pool. You're trying out.

C'mon, Coach, you can't make us.
I thought this was a free country, Coach.
Get in.

Bree, if you try out, too, I'll give you extra credit.
That'll raise your C to a B.

What's it gonna be, Bree?

Oh no! I assumed I was done with self-doubt...!
THEY'RE GONNA LAUGH AT YOU!
DO PALMS SWEAT UNDER-WATER?

MAYBE THIS POOL IS HARDER TO SWIM IN THAN THE COMMUNITY POOL?
MAYBE MS. ETTA WAS JUST BEING NICE AND YOU'RE NOT READY?

Come on, Bree. You know how to swim now.

NO WAY.
YOU'RE IN DEEP NOW.
HOW WILL YOU GET OUT OF THIS?
NO HOW.

IS IT TOO LATE TO HIDE IN THE LIBRARY?
TOO-OOOO-OOO LATE.

I'm going to die of embarrassment.
EMBAR-RAAAAS-SED
Probably.
Just try not to come in last.
WHA IF YOu FORG HOW TO FLOA
TOOO-OOOOO MUCH.
WHERE?

AH! AH!
Aaaaaaaaaaand GO!
AH! THEY STARTED!
TRY NOT TO COME IN LAST!
IT'S SO FAR.

IS IT DEEPER THAN THE OTHER POOL?

HOW FAR DOWN DID YOU DIVE?
ARE YOU EVEN MOVING FORWARD?
I can't get away from them! They're everywhere!
GONNA COME IN LAST.
THE OTHER SWIMMERS ARE PROBABLY ALREADY DONE.
YOU CAN'T GET AWAY.
THIS WATER IS COLD!
WHICH WAY?
THIS IS WACK GIRL MAGIC.
STILL IN MY LANE?

PADDLE.
Watch your form.
Stay calm.
OH NO.
AM I THERE YET?
I'M SO OVER THIS.

Maybe I can outswim these thoughts!
ARE YOU TIRED ALREADY?
WHEN IS THIS OVER?

WISH I GOT MATH PUZZLES.
You're in control.
ARMS TIRED YET?
LEGS TIRED YET?
YOU SHOULD QUIT NOW.
YOU STILL GOING?
DIDN'T SWALLOW WATER.
NOT FAST ENOUGH.
ARE YOU KICKING RIGHT?
WISH IT WAS LUNCH ALREADY.
WANNA GO HOME

WANNA.
BREATHE.

Almost there!

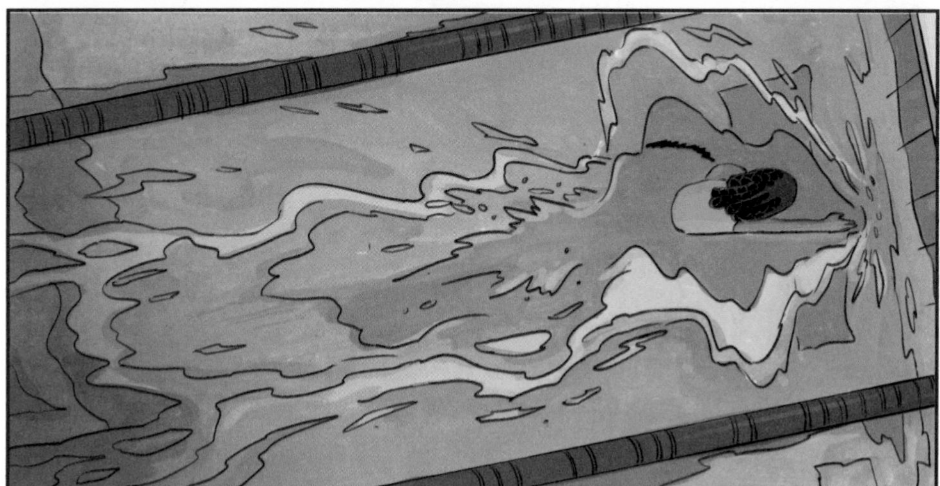

>INHALE<

Where is everyone?

Bree, you came in first!

What the—

That was... fun!

Good.
Very good,
Bree.

You made
the cut.
What?

See you here
for practice.
3:15 p.m. tomorrow.
Let's make sure
that wasn't
a **FLUKE.**

But I don't wanna be on the
swim team!
Do I?!

Clara's
on the swim
team!
Plus their uniforms
are pretty cool!
Yeah, that's
RIGHT!

But I already
planned to sign up
for math
club.

Pretty sure my dad would prefer me joining that.
Maybe.
Or maybe he'll come to see you at swim meets.
Seeing you swim can be your NEW new routine.
GO, BREE, GO!
GO, BREE, GO!
That would be really cool!
Right?! Besides, you should've seen your face after the race. You had fun!
The real question is, what do YOU want to do?
Humberto, get in the pool! You're next!

It's time for club sign-up for second semester.

WELCOME 2 MATH CLUB
On one hand, I'd do great in math club.

On the other hand...
MATH

Swimming still scares me. But when I swim REAL FAST, I don't overthink.
And maybe Dad will come to all my races.
Plus racing was really fun...

But what scares me more than swimming is disappointing Dad.
MATH CLUB
SWIM TEAM

After school
Dad, could you—
Bree...

Why is Clara staring through our window?

Could you sign my permission slip?
Ah, math club sign-up for next semester!

Actually, I thought I'd try something NEW.
Ah, thinking science club, then?

"Swim team"?!

Haven't you spent enough time on swimming this semester?
I thought it might be fun to compete.

Well, this isn't what I was... expecting.

So long as it doesn't affect your studies...
I promise it won't, Dad!

EEEEEEEE!!!

We're going to be on the swim team together, Bree!!

>Sigh<

The next day
Clara, this is a mistake. Everyone will know so much more than me.
They may have more experience...
but most of them are self-taught, like me. You had a really good teacher, Bree.

Wanna learn how to do a flip turn?
What's a flip turn?

When you swim to the far wall, you do a FLIP. Then push off the wall with your feet, giving you a little boost on the swim back.
That sounds like fun!

It is!

We use flip turns and open turns in longer races, depending on what stroke we're doing. And for the relay medley.
You SPIN and push off the... Actually it's easier if I SHOW you.

Now you try!

Okay!

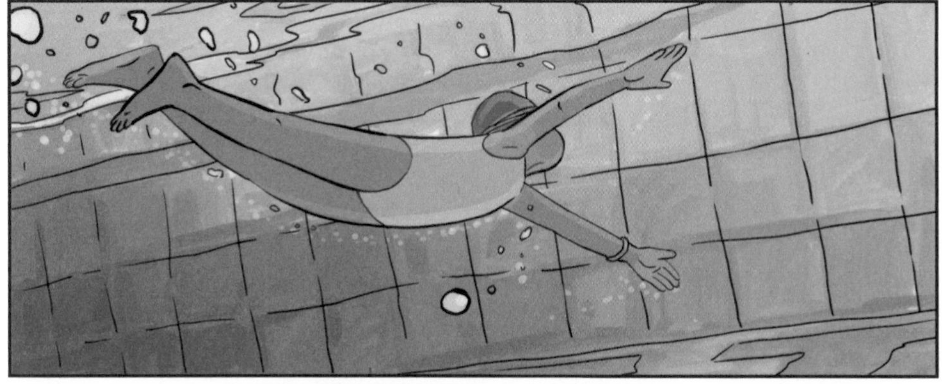

BONK!

YOWCH!!!
You'll get it. We'll keep practicing.

Hey, Clara...

...Check the ink.
Is it real?
No, but it gets the point across.
REAL TUFF
That's Phillipa. She's a strong swimmer.
Just...don't call her the Anchor...
Why would I call her that?

Just don't. She chased the last girl who did for, like, four blocks.

You're new, right?

psych!
You're **TOAST** if you ruin our season.

And don't mess up our relay medley.

Tracey! What's up, girl?!
RUDE... What's a "relay medley" anyway?

You know a relay race, where a runner passes on the baton to the next runner?
Yeah.

It's like that, but with swimming. And no baton.
Four swimmers, each swimming a different style:

Butterfly

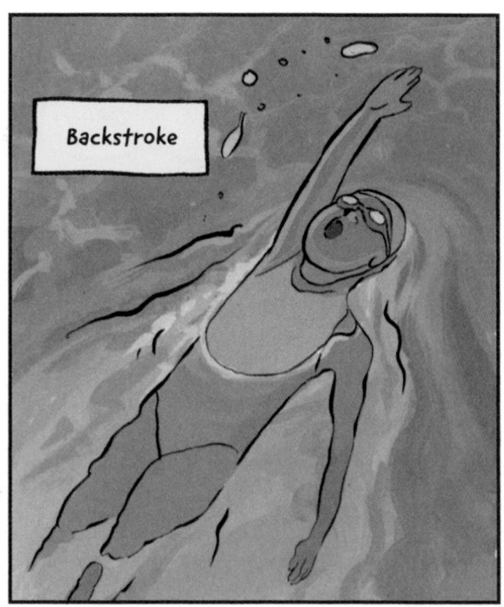
Backstroke

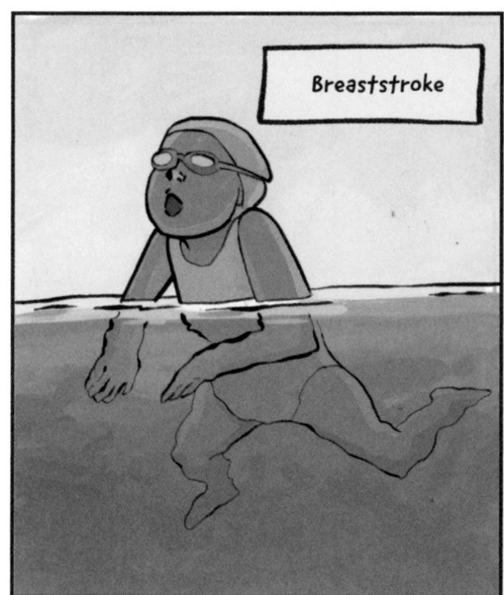
Breaststroke

And freestyle
First team to finish wins

It's a real team effort. The best relay teams are in sync, in the pool and out.
CANNONBALL!

WOOOOOo o o!

SPLASH

>Gluck<

Oh, **THAT'S** why they call her the Anchor!

Who said that?!

Who **SAID** that?!
Phillipa, stop goofing off!

>Sigh<
We don't stand a chance.

5

Go, Manatees!

Race day!
Congrats on making the team.
I'll try to make it to your race!
-Dad

SWIM MEET #1
Green Lakes Middle
Home of the Sensational Stingrays

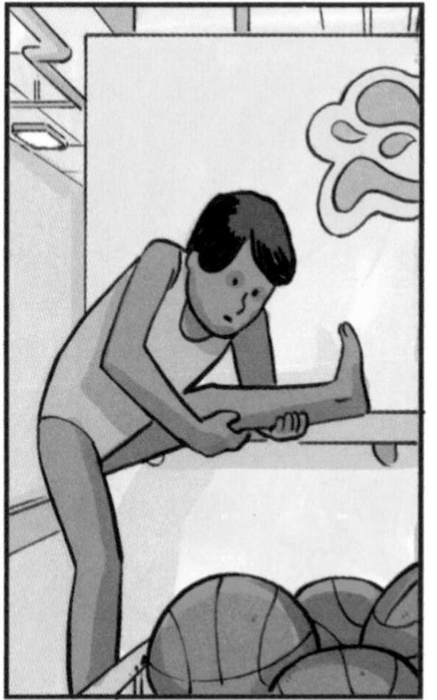

Ms. Etta!
You came!

I had to come see you swim! I wouldn't miss it!
Thank you!

Etta?
The same "Etta" who taught Bree to swim?

I looked you up! What a great swimming career!
You should help me coach. Bree's teammates could use the help.
That's very kind—

No, seriously.

Listen, the district wants to close our pool.
A good swim season might change their minds.
Ours is the only free pool open to everyone in the community during non-school hours.

Oh...I just came to watch Bree swim today...
RACERS, APPROACH THE LINE!!
Sorry, I didn't mean to put you on the spot!

You should get back to the team!
Yikes!
You're right! Think about it, okay?!

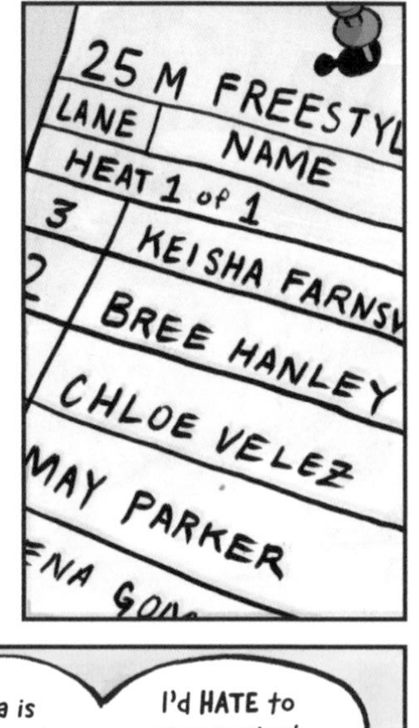
25 M FREESTYL
LANE
NAME
HEAT 1 of 1
3
KEISHA FARNSV
2
BREE HANLEY
CHLOE VELEZ
MAY PARKER

You're racing Keisha?

Keisha is really good.
I'd HATE to race against her!

Phillipa, build up Bree's confidence...
...Don't smush it.
I'm just sayin'...

...She swims with grace and power. Her technique is second to none!
Don't believe it, Bree. ANYONE can be beat.

Ha ha! Look, it's Kiddie Pool!

Don't listen to them, Bree.
I DON'T BELONG HERE.
I'LL MAKE A FOOL OF MYSELF.
I'LL LET THE SCHOOL DOWN.

Breathe.

You're not in the kiddie pool anymore.
Watch and learn how the BIG KIDS swim!

TWEEET!
AND GO!

And our racers are off to a fiery start in the 25-meter freestyle!

The home-team swimmer takes a commanding lead!

With all others close behind!

Here they come!

It'll be close!

Approaching the
wall our winner
will be...

1ST
The swimmer from Green Lakes Middle!

2ND
Gulf Shrimp Middle comes in second.

3RD
In third, the swimmer from Enith Brigitha in her very first race!

She did it?! Bree came in third!

4TH
And in fourth, a disappointing finish for the swimmer from Holyoke.
Her coach is not going to be happy about that.

HOORAY, BREE!

Don't get overconfident. You've got two more races today.
But my arms feel like spaghetti...

Keisha, let's talk after the meet...

C'mon, everybody, we're on a roll!

Brigitha's early promise slips away with a fifth-place finish in the 50-meter breaststroke.

Our former third-place finisher comes in eighth in the 50-meter backstroke.

Maybe I spoke too soon. Let me know when it's safe to look.

Brigitha strikes back!

1ST
Clara takes first in the 50-meter butterfly...

And the 25-meter backstroke!

Clara does it again!
1ST

Great job, Clara!

Hmmm...

A fabulous day of racing.
Congrats to our top racers!
1
2
3
4

After the meet

Humberto. Have you seen my dad?
Huh? No, why?

Oh.
No reason.

You'll get 'em next time, Phillipa.
Yeah... probably not.

I gotta get better, or I'll lose my spot.

What's that all about?
Coach, I'm sorry—
"Sorry" doesn't win races.

You're cut.
What?!

Keisha, get your things and leave! At Holyoke, we only want WINNERS.

But everyone has a bad meet sometimes!

Coach, please! All I want to do is swim!
Then do it somewhere else.

Let this be a lesson to the rest of you.

Winning is the **ONLY** option at Holyoke.

And I'll **HAVE** winners on this team, one way or another.

Coach?
Yeah...?

I didn't make Bree a good swimmer.
It was already in her.

It's in all of your girls. I can see it.
But you need to believe it so they can, too.

Are they really taking away the pool?
They're thinking of putting a Smoothie Palace in its place.
Those ARE pretty good smoothies...

But we can't let them take away pool access, like when I was a girl...
I won't let that happen again.
!
MIDDL
So you'll help?!

I'm IN, Coach. Let's turn this team around.

Dad! Dad! Look at what I won!

Sorry Bree,
I had to work late
and couldn't make it
today. I'll try for
next time
-Dad

Next time!

The next day
Hi, Clara. Get anything good?
Let's find out.

What's wrong?

I...I'll see you tomorrow, okay?
Clara?

Oh, okay.

Upstairs

We are happy to inform you that your daughter CLARA has been accepted into Holyoke Preparatory Academy for next year on a swimming scholarship. Acceptance pending results of an academic entrance exam, in the area of mathematics.

6

Ripple Effect

Team practice
RUB RUB
I don't think I've ever been awake this early.
SCROLL SCROLL
I definitely haven't.
Okay, girls. You wanna win?
I do, too!

So we're adding some firepower to the training program.

Ms. Etta will be helping me coach you.
She was a swimmer here and her team even made it to State.
From now on, we'll practice every morning as well as after school.
Etta?

Good morning, girls.
We'll start with the basics and add to it little by little.

TWEETT

Let's start by building your endurance!

Again!
Strength!

Speed!

Again!

Let's work on that form!
Bree, keep those kicks at the surface!

Clara, my legs are DEAD.
I would cry if I hadn't already sweated out my TEARS.

Again!

SWIM MEET #2
Alligator Way Middle
Home of the
Golden Gators
ALLIGATOR WAY

We started getting better.

Sloooowly...
But surely.

You can do it!

After the meet

SCHOOL

What's up, Bree?
I think a storm is coming. A big one.

Who wants ice-cream floats?!
YAAAY!!!

That went pretty well!
The individual races, sure.

But the medley is in bad shape. The girls need more one-on-one training.
But there's only two of us, Etta!

Ice cream!!
Heh heh!

DINE

>Sigh< Guess we'll just have to make it work.
What else can we do?

Pray for a miracle?

But that's a problem for another day.
You coming? This place is famous for its floats.
You go ahead!

Next day at school
HOME OF THE
MIGHTY MANATE

Can you help me with my math homework tonight?
Those pesky integers tripping you up?
Always.

What's going on over here?

Oh NO!
Bree! LOOK!!

KEISHA?
What's SHE doing here?!
I dunno...

But I'm worried it has something to do with the swim team...

At afternoon practice
Girls, we have some very exciting news!

We have a new **transfer student**. Some of you may already know her...

Give a warm swim team welcome to **KEISHA**!

Thanks, Coach P. I promise I'll lead this...team... to victory.
Someone has to.

"Lead this team"? How dare she?!
She's funny.
All right, everyone in the pool!

Moments later
Word is, when she was kicked off Holyoke's team, Brigitha was the only other team with open spots.

So she transferred here. I think to SPY on us.

All Keisha cares about is winning a medal at State.
She doesn't care about our team.

What stroke does she compete in?
Breaststroke is her strongest. But she can do it all.

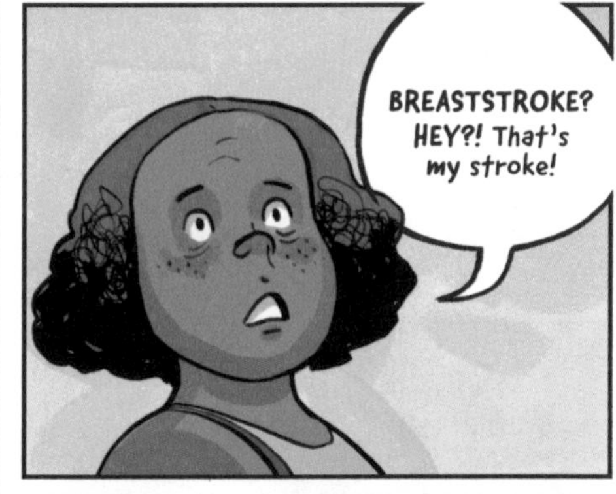

BREASTSTROKE? HEY?! That's my stroke!

Heh heh heh...
Get used to riding the BENCH.
With Keisha here, your days in the pool are numbered.

Now for a post-workout snack!
CANDY
rippp...
Is that a candy bar?!

Heh heh.
Hey!
I never eat sweets. You ARE what you eat, Bree.
SLAP!

ELITE swimmers eat a proper diet of salad, carbs, and protein!

Ugh... You beat me by luck in our race.
That's SO obvious now.

Where y'all headed to?
The park, Keisha.
The park?

Home is where you should go. To study and rest!
>Sigh< See you at practice tomorrow.

Wow, Keisha has the best advice! The team's chances of going to State just went up by a **bazillion**!

Ugh...she's unbearable.
And boring.

But she's a good swimmer **AND** your teammate now... She could be nicer but she has good advice.

You want to win, right?

SWIM MEET #3
Hurricane Bay Middle
Home of the
Salty Sandpipers

Here ya go, Keisha. Your race assignments.

You sure you can handle three races?
I've got you covered, Coach.

Coach! I didn't see my name on the lane sheet?

Sorry, Phillipa, I've already assigned all the spots.
You'll have to sit this race day out.

I understand, Coach.

What's that?
You mean the diving block?

Oh no! You've probably never used of one those before, have you?!
COAACH!!

You didn't tell her about the blocks?!
We never got this far in competition before. I forgot the rest of the schools use diving blocks!

Diving Block Crash Course!
Position your legs like a sprinter.
Dive in with minimal splash, then streamline.

But don't dive straight down or you'll dive too DEEP.

And not too straight out or you'll BELLY FLOP.
What's a belly flop?

Don't belly flop. Don't belly flop. Don't belly flop.
Whatever that is...

TWEEET!

FLOP

OooOOoooo

Ow, my FACE hurts!

The race started...
And before you knew it, it was over.

1
1
2
3
1st Place:
Clara
25-meter
Butterfly
1st Place:
Keisha
50-meter
Backstroke
2nd Place:
Bree
25-meter
Freestyle
3rd Place:
Enith Brigitha
Middle
Medley

Good swimming today, Keisha. Truce?

Yeah, okay.
TRUCE.

No luck, huh?

I'm sure he'll make it to the next one.
Me too.

7

Pushing Off

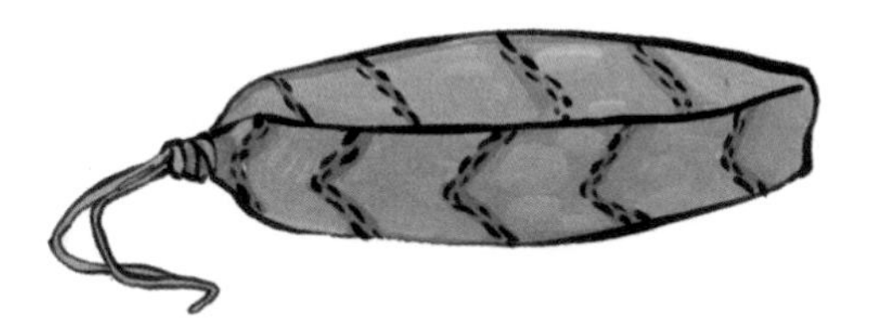

A few days later
Check out the new diving block!
It was donated anonymously by someone at the bank.

SPLASH

Much better, Bree!
Does she ever give up? She's been at it all morning.

This week is division finals. If we do well, we go to State!
And it's all gonna come down to the medley.
Exactly.
CHILE
PLEASE

Bree won't really help us in the medley anyway.
So who cares how she does?

She's getting better every day, Keisha!
Face it...our medley ain't it. Best to just get a solo medal.

Don't mind her. Wanna take a break?
No.

I'm gonna keep at it.

I wanna try, too!
This should be fun to watch. You can't even float.

It's not a floating competition, SPY!
SPLOOSH

I'm not a spy!
Well, you're not one of US.
SPLASH!
Girls!

GIRLS!! Stop it!!

Start supporting each other or you've got zero chance of winning!

My middle school swim team wasn't beaten in the pool.
We lost because we didn't all stand together, and that—
Ms. Etta?

What is it, Phillipa?

She started it.

After practice
Great move upsetting Ms. Etta, Phillipa.

Ms. Etta's right. We need to get better if we wanna get to State.

The problem is, Holyoke keeps crushing everybody.
Well, like any math problem...
Let's break down their winning formula into steps. Starting with...
How does Holyoke train?

Why are y'all looking at **ME**?

'Cause you **TRAINED** there, genius.
You expect me to remember **everything** we did?

Tell us everything, spy! Spill!
We should just see for **ourselves.**

You mean...
We **INFILTRATE!**

We'll be the spies! Like Keisha!
This is going to be fun!

I'm having no part of this.
Like I said, you're not one of US.

But how are we gonna get in without school uniforms?

I know just the guy who can help us...
Heh heh.

Soon
No way! Being head costume designer is a sacred duty.

Please, Humberto, we need to borrow the costumes from your rich private school play.
We just need them for the afternoon.

We'll return them in sterling condition. We promise!
C'mon, Humberto, don't be a weenie.

I'm not a weenie.
Ya know... it'd be an honor to be dressed by one of our school's great artists.

You've seen our plays?
Your costumes are the **highlight** of every school play.
I never miss 'em. I even **reserved** a seat.

PHILLIPA

PHILLIPA! That's vandalism!
BREE! I don't obey laws that I can't **SPELL.**

Just this afternoon?
You have my word.

Okay, but I'm going with you to make sure they stay **pristine.**

Costume room
Let's see...
CLICK

We're counting on you, Humberto. Do your best work.
Oh, Clara...

I do my absolute best every time.

And so
What's the plan again?
Simple.
We'll bus over, sneak in, and watch some of their practice.

Keisha, what are YOU doing here?!
You don't stand a chance of getting in without me.

DONUTS!
SMECK
These aren't for you!

I thought you hated sweets.
I DO. These aren't for me, either.

We're taking the BUS?!! Wait a minute, let me call my driver!!
No time to waste. Are you IN or OUT, Keisha?
27 HOLYOKE VIA STR
Transit

The things I do for this team.

A little later
Team...

KRA-KOOM!
We're here.
HOLYOKE

Oh no, they've got a school guard! What now?!

I've got this.

Hello, Security Guard Kevin.
Keisha... I thought you weren't attending here anymore—

Do I smell a Sugar Craze© Premium Donut?
SNIFF SNIFF
It's a WHOLE BOX of Sugar Craze© Donuts!

I can't eat all this yummy tasty sugariness myself. Want some?

Well...I suppose I can take a few off your hands, heh heh.

Aren't you going to have any?

Yes. Of course. I...love sugary sweets...

They're worth EVERY cavity!
tremble
YUMMY

ENRICH YOUR LEARNING
ENRICH LEARNING
ENRICH LEARNING
EXIT

Where to now?
I was here for a swimming class once.

Are you new here?
The pool is this way!
I hope those aren't our new uniforms.

HOME
Whoa.

Wow, they've got an **indoor** pool?!
In Florida?!
It's newly tiled, too.

How do they afford this? Do they have better bake sales than us or something?
No, Phillipa, they're just rich.
I think those donuts are making me sick.

We're so outmatched.

Who are you guys pretending to be? **Winners?**

Well, you lose at that, too. Those costumes **SUCK.**
Hey!

Nice pool, huh?

Do you miss it, Keisha?

We don't care how nice your pool is, Tinsley.

What did you say, Kiddie Pool?
Trash talk won't save you at race time!

We're going to State...
...and we're going to win!
HA!

We're going to out-train you. And outswim you.
'Cause fancy pools and "nice" equipment won't give you the heart of a...

MANATEE!

I was going to say "champion."
Yeah, but our mascot's the manatee.
Aren't you the Anchor?

"Why?" you ask. 'Cause she sinks like a boat anchor.
BLOOOP!
What did you call me?!

Not just me. EVERYONE calls you that!
Probably even your "friends".
HEY!

You girls don't belong here. It's time for you to go.

Clara?!
I didn't see you there.

Your mother worked hard to get you into our program next year.

Are you serious?!
No WAY!

Don't blow it by pulling these stunts with this...
"crowd."
We're taking a chance on you...

Don't embarrass us like Keisha did.
Now, please leave...
We're starting practice.

Back outside
You're leaving us?!

Yes. Well...not yet. I still need to pass the math exam.

Now who's the spy? Good-girl Clara has been lying to us the whole time!
I didn't lie!
Oh? Then what would you call it?

And I'm sick of you guys calling me the Anchor behind my back!
Well, I'm sick of you taking everything as a joke! Holding my team BACK!

YOUR team?!
Yeah, my team. You can't come in here and start shot calling!

How is it your team if you're plotting to leave?

STOP IT! All of you! We should be friends, but we're barely even a team.
I should have never joined.
We have Regionals tomorrow. Let's just focus on that.

Phillipa, did you get a stain on your costume?
Umm...
No?

All right kids, last stop.

SWIM MEET #6
Regionals
Sawgrass Prospect Middle
The Tenacious Tiger Sharks

EB

I can't help it if I don't float well. I have a lot of muscle.

Seen my dad, Humberto?

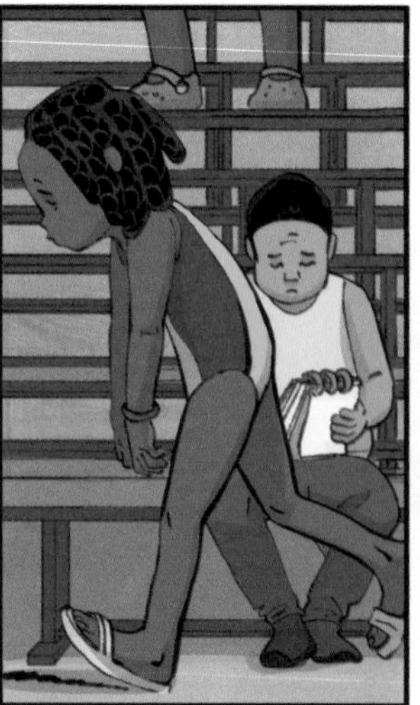

I didn't think so.

Bree! There's something I want to give you.

This is the photo of my middle school team. The one I made a puzzle of.

I want you to have it... Always remember winning is important, but friends and community are even more important.

Being your coach helped me remember that.
But our team is always arguing.

We did, too! Teammates argue sometimes.

But if you stick together, you won't fall apart.

What if we already have?

25-meter freestyle
...Get set...
JUDGES

Go!

And an EXPLOSIVE start for the swimmer from Brigitha!

A powerful finish!
1ST

She doesn't seem too happy, though...

Relay medley
The Tiger Sharks are fending off an inspired challenge from the Manatees! Which team will go to the State Championships?!
JUDGES

GO!

JUDGES

You're on the breaststroke leg of the medley.
So watch that open turn, Bree.
Are you okay? You seem upset... Bree?

Don't mess up the turn, Bree.

Looks like Bree...

...is a little too far from the wall.
weak
grip

weak
pushhh
Not a strong push-off as a result.

But she's making up for it with sheer effort.

Now for the last leg!

A veeery
close finish!

Let's go to
the judges.
CLICK!

It's come down to the wire...
Our judges check the times.
JUDGES

Congratulations,
Enith Brigitha—
you're going
to the
State
Championship!

WE DID IT!

...WE'RE GOING TO STATE!

YANK!

I quit.

Back at home

3

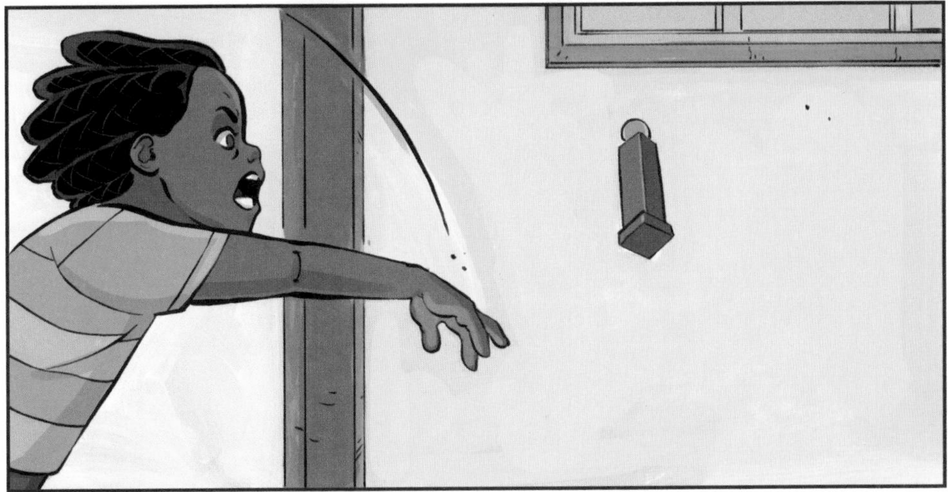

CRASH!

Whoa, what's going on?!

Would it have killed you to come to ONE of my meets?

Bree... I'm sorry. I got delayed again by—

You'd rather spend time at work than with me.
Bree, that's not true.

I admit, working two jobs has been a handful. But I do it to give us a better life.

You don't like that I joined the swim team. Now Clara's leaving, too.

So I have no dad
AND no best friend.
That's enough of that talk, Bree.

Well, you win, I QUIT!

You quit?
I'm sorry I disappointed you.

Swim Sisters

The week of State
Class, what's one way to solve hard problems?
Bree?

By working backward?
That's correct!
MATH
PEMDAS

MANATEES
#1
STATE!

Quote for the school paper, Keisha?
About the swim team going to State...
OFFICE

I knew we'd make it to State all along.
With me on the team it was a SURE THING.

Will Bree quitting make it harder?
BEFORE YOU SPEAK THINK
No. It won't.
Tsk... Same old Keisha.

Hi, Bree.

Haylie?!! I'm not skipping class...
I'm your biggest fan! You're such a great swimmer and...
GO NATEES

Because of you I started taking lessons, too.
I didn't know how to swim either.

I hope you rejoin the team.
OFFICE

I'm making all your favorites tonight, Bree!
Beans! Rice! Plantains...
Are you listening?

I GOT IT!
I solved my puzzle!
CLICK!

Congrats.
Now set the table.

So...you're not going back to the team?
Nope! This is the life!
No more early morning drills.

No more practice. Or bickering. Or thrill of victory.
Or Clara.
Besides, I think they're still mad at me.

Bree, there's something I should tell you...

I don't know how to swim.

It's true. I almost drowned as a kid, and I've been scared of the water ever since.
!

I didn't come to your meets because pools make me **nervous.**

Even though I know **you're** safe in the pool.
It's silly, but I can't help it.

Just know, every time you swim without fear, it makes me very happy.

I'm so proud of you.
Thanks, Dad.

It's up to you if you don't want to rejoin the team. But stay in touch with your old teammates.

Because they're not just teammates—they're your friends, and everyone needs friends.

You can't spend ALL your time on puzzles. Heck, even a puzzle lover like Ms. Etta would tell you that.

Wait, that's it! **THE MISSING PIECE!!!**

Dad, I think you just helped me solve **another** puzzle!

Ah-HA!

Dad! You're a genius!
Why, yes. Yes, of course I am...
Why am I a genius?

Etta's missing pieces are her **FRIENDS!**
You talking about her puzzles?

Yes and no...
The relay medley is a puzzle she can't solve on her own.

Dad, can we go to the bank?
The bank?
Why?! Do you need a loan?
I'll explain on the way!
hop!
hop!

BANK
Good to see you again, Mr. Hanley...

LOANS
How can I help you?
My daughter has a puzzle that you might be a piece of...

Is this you, Ms. Yvette?
ONLINE
NO FEES

YVETTE JOHNSON
Relay Medley: Backstroke

Yes... But where...? How did you get that photo?!

I got it from your old teammate Ms. Etta. She needs you. She needs her old team.

Okay, you and your dad follow me.
The dentist?!
We're going to the dentist.

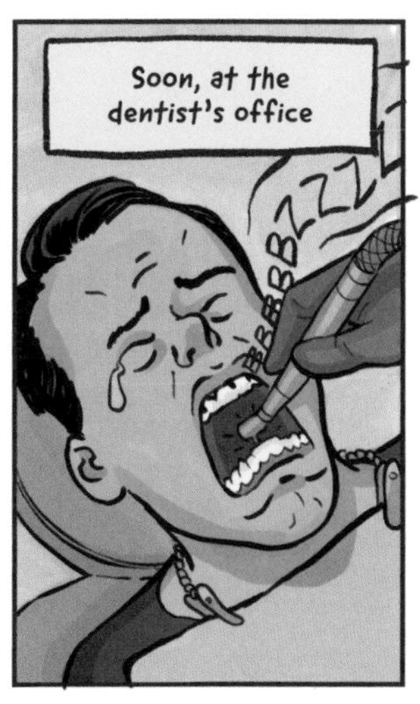
Soon, at the dentist's office
BBBBZZZZ

Yvette?! Is that you?
Dwhas dgoing dwon?

Etta's in trouble and needs our help!

DR. JAMIE BENDROSS
Relay Medley: Breast-stroke

Sorry, Mr. Franklin. We'll finish this later.
Dwhy does dthis always dhappen to me..?

What about—you know—the **other** person on our team..?
What if Etta doesn't want to see her?

Swim sisters forever, right?
I guess...

What if they aren't comfortable talking to each other after what went down?
What went down?

WHAT WENT DOWN

We had the fiercest team in the state. I had a mean breaststroke. Yvette had a solid backstroke.
Ahem.

My backstroke was **exquisite.**

Etta was dominant in the front crawl.
And Mari had excellent butterfly technique.

It was a miracle season. We did **everything together**... and that was the **problem.**
SWIM SISTERS!

One day, Mari invited us to a pool in her **other friends'** neighborhood.

Mari's older cousin, Monica, drove us there. We were so excited!
Hi, Mari!

The man at the entrance let Mari and her friends in, but when it was our turn to enter...
This pool ain't for you.
?

Excuse me?
You don't live **here**. You got some ID?

This is a public pool! **We're** the **public!**
Sir, we're together. I don't live in this neighborhood either.

Mari, are you coming or what?
Yeah, I wanna get a deck chair before they're taken.

Sir...
MARI!!!
Young lady, let me handle this...

Do I have to call the POLICE?

Mari?

Mari left us high and dry.

Now BEAT IT!

Our clothes were still in Monica's car. It took three buses to get home.

The next morning was State. Mari didn't show up.
Without her, we couldn't compete in the medley. I know we would have won.

That's a shame.
How do we find Mari?

She—
I figured out who she is!

She runs the **DINER**!

Yvette? Jamie?...

What are you doing here?

Did something happen to Etta?

Ms. Etta and the school need you.

I'm on the swim team.
Etta got us to State, but just like back then, she needs help from her team.

What if she doesn't want my help?
Then you'll have to convince her.

A puzzle needs every piece for it to work. We need **everyone** to chip in.

You don't want to be the missing piece again, do you?
I...I... I don't know?

I don't know if Etta will forgive you.
But for any chance of that...

You'll have to take the plunge.
Get it, Dad?
Oh jeez, Bree...

Let's go. The old teammates have some catching up to do.

DING DONG
Who could that be?

Hello?

How's it going, champ?!

Oh my goodness—

Yvette!
Jamie!
It's so good to see you!

Mari?

What is SHE doing here?

Sorry. This was a mistake.
turn

Etta, I'm sorry about what happened.
I turned my back on the team and on doing the RIGHT THING.

...No, not this time...

I knew it was wrong...
But I took the easy way out and just went along with it.

I apologize for what I did, Etta.

I'm sorry, Yvette. I'm sorry, Jamie. I messed up.
And I miss you.

It's been fifty years, but in my heart, we're still a team and always will be.

Now that you've gotten the team back to State, let us help you get them over the finish line.

I won't let you or the school down again.

What do you say, Etta? Swim sisters?

>Sigh<

Swim sisters.

Okay. Let's finish what we **STARTED!**

The next day at school
LIBRARY
NEW

Clara?

Hi.
H-hi.

What are you studying?
The math part of my entrance exam. Y'know, super-easy stuff.
So, so easy.

Actually, I'm kinda WORRIED...
I can help! Scoot over.

I'll never figure this stuff out...
Sure you will! You can do it!

Clara, I'm sorry I quit the team. I thought you'd leave and we wouldn't be friends anymore.

NEVER! I don't care what school I'm going to. You're my best friend, Bree. Always.
Always?
ALWAYS.

Still have my friendship bracelet?
Absolutely do!

When's the exam?
This weekend.
Then we've got a lot of work to do!

And so
Bree?
LIBRARY

We heard what you did for the team...and for Miss Etta. That was pretty cool.

Whoever said you were selfish was wrong.
Who said I was **SELFISH?!**

Me...

Sorry I bailed on the team.

And I'm sorry I doubted you, Keisha.
You ate a box of sugary **donuts** for us.

I guess I like you guys more than I **hate** sugary donuts.

I'm sorry, too.
Me too.
Yeah.

A team is like a family.
Sometimes family shows you how to do a flip turn.
Or tells funny jokes
And is a little annoying.

Will you take me back on the team?

Depends... Which leg of the medley are you hoping for?

OWWW! All right, ALL RIGHT!
BUMP

Bree, will you please rejoin the team?

My dad says one butterfly can change the weather. I say four butterflies can change the world.
"Swim sisters" on three...

One...
Two...
Three...
MANATEES!
SWIM SISTERS!!

That afternoon
Girls, we have a lot of work to do before Saturday...

...and not much time. But between me, Coach Pinella, and your new coaches...

We have decades' worth of swimming knowledge at your disposal!

Let's get STARTED!

ENDURANCE.

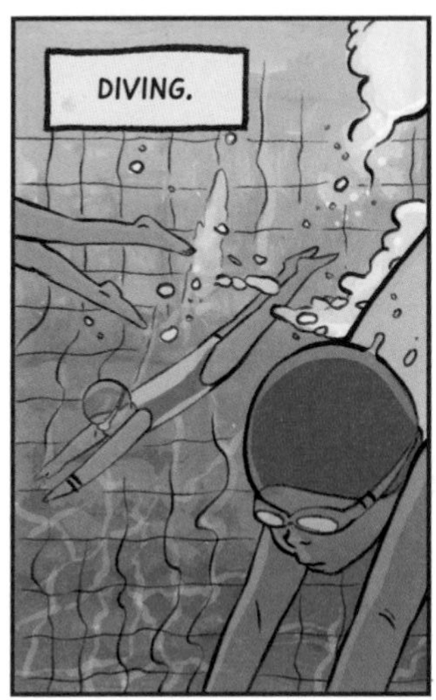
DIVING.

SPEED.
Very good. We're getting there.

What's wrong, Phillipa?
I...I can't float so good.

The other kids goof on me. They call me the Anchor.

Or maybe it's because you're the Anchor of the team, keeping everyone in good spirits, even during the toughest training sessions.
You keep the team from drifting apart.

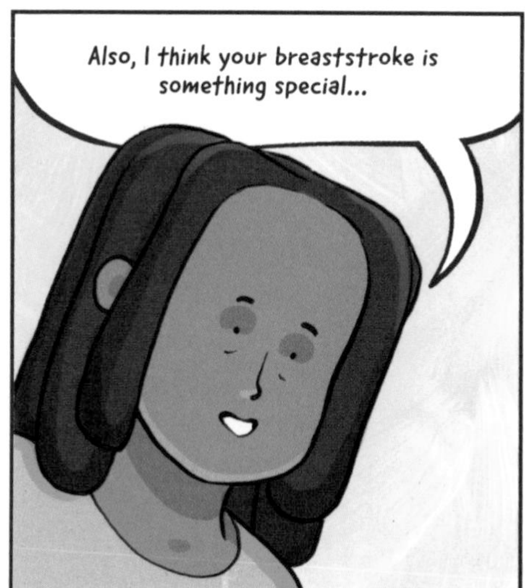
Also, I think your breaststroke is something special...

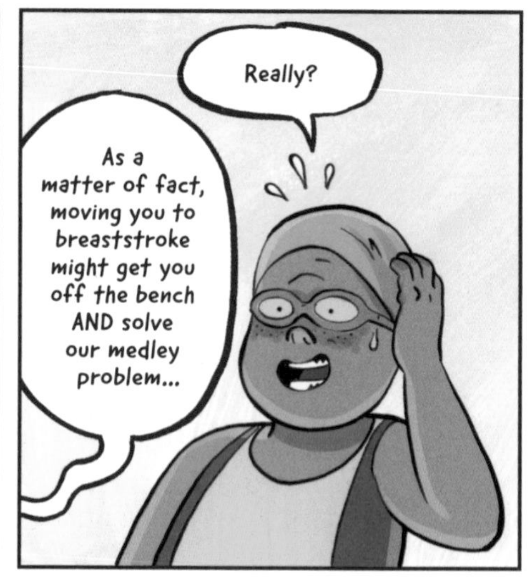
Really?
As a matter of fact, moving you to breaststroke might get you off the bench AND solve our medley problem...

9

State

Sorry I can't make it today, sweetie.
It's okay, Dad.
POOL RULES

Today is final presentations at my program.
I understand. Really.

Good luck today, Bree.
You too!

Go out there and swim laps around 'em!
smooch.

WOOOOO-HOOOO!!
Etta's ready to go!
Manatee pride!

STATE CHAMPIONSHIPS
Holyoke Prep School Home of the Heck-Raising Herons
HOLYOKE
rub rub
peel
Swim fans!...
Welcome the best middle school swim teams in the state of Florida!

The crowd is bursting with excitement, so let's not wait a minute more!
MANATEES
HOLYOKE
HOLYOKE
H

Tinsley...
Keisha...
I would say "It's good to see you."

But that would be a lie.

You ready, Keisha?
Completely.

The races start
TWEEEEET

INDIVIDUAL TRIUMPH!

PERSONAL GLORY!

UNTIL...

A great day of races! Our teams gave it their all!
NOW the deciding event of today's meet:
THE RELAAAAY MEDLEEYY!!!

Keisha, we need your strong start at backstroke. Gonna put Phillipa on breaststroke. That all right?

I got you, Coach. The breaststroke is in good hands with Phillipa.

Clara, you're up third. We need your technical ability in the fly and...

Bree, last leg. Your never-give-up attitude will bring us home!

All right, team. You know what to do.

Etta, any last words of wisdom?

Have FUN!

Our swimmers approach the blocks...

And get into position...

exhale

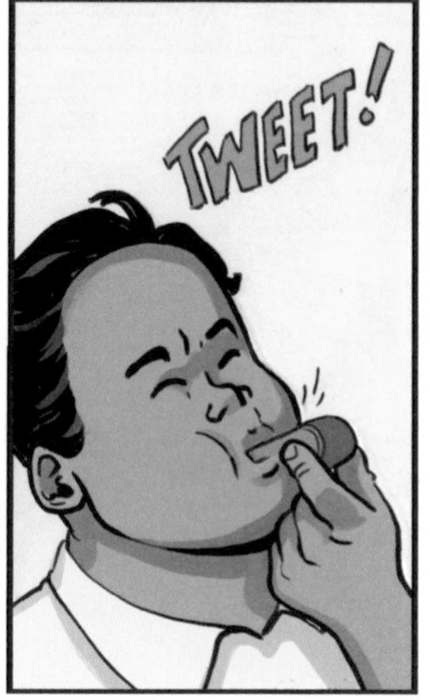
TWEET!

And they're off to
a mighty start!

Great form and
speed on display, here in
the backstroke.

We'd expect nothing less from the
teams competing here today.

The first to approach the wall, it's the upstarts from Brigitha.

Watch that dive, Phillipa!
Can they hold on in the second leg?

SPLOOSH!

Oooooooooo...

Garrrbble...
Not a great dive.

Holyoke takes advantage and shows
why they win the medley every year.

Brigitha has
fallen behind. Is their
chance over?

Do it,
Clara!
We'll find out on the
butterfly leg.

FLY!

Last leg, Kiddie Pool, you ready?
You sound SCARED, Tinsley.

Huh? No way...

Excuse me...
Excuse me, pardon me...
Dad?!

Dad, you made it!!
GO, BREE, GO!!!

Oops!

FLIP!

That's better.
GO BREE!

Here comes Clara!
I got it! I'm ready! I think...

See ya later, Kiddie Pool!
Holyoke begins their last leg, can anyone challenge them?

Brigitha comes in strong...
...And they've got heart!

GO, BREE!!!

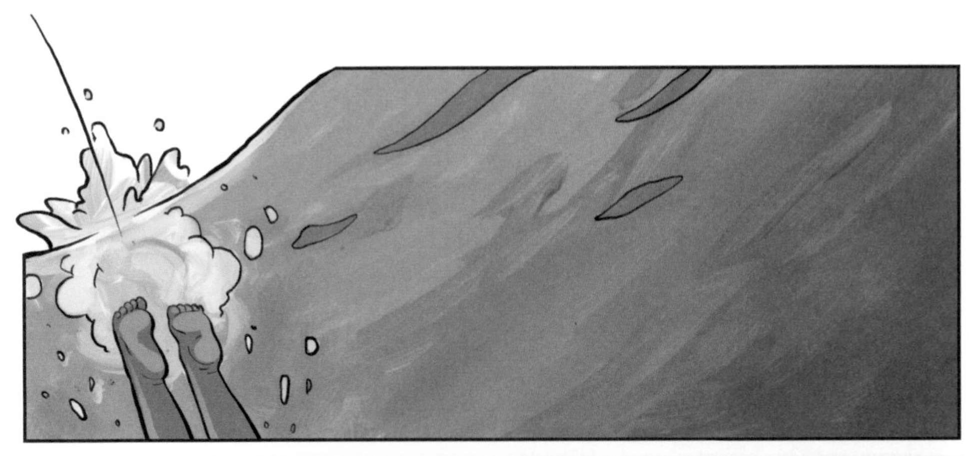

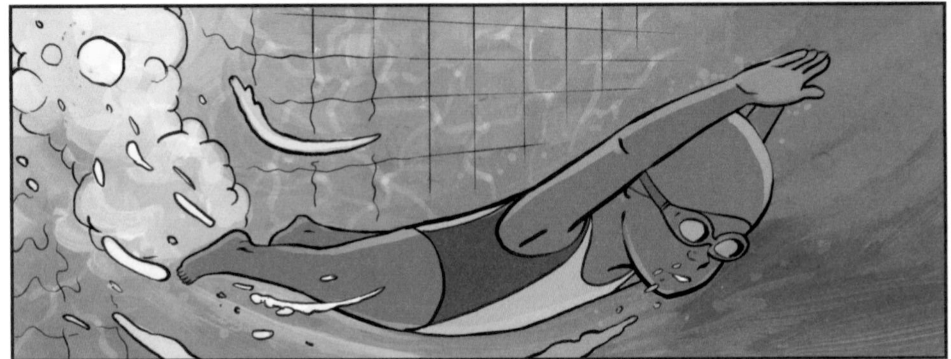

And heeere comes Brigitha!

Wow! She's REALLY good!

Surprisingly strong start for Brigitha, but Holyoke still leads.

Oh no! She's had problems with turns all season!
YANK!

SPLOOSH
Stay calm. And... NOW!

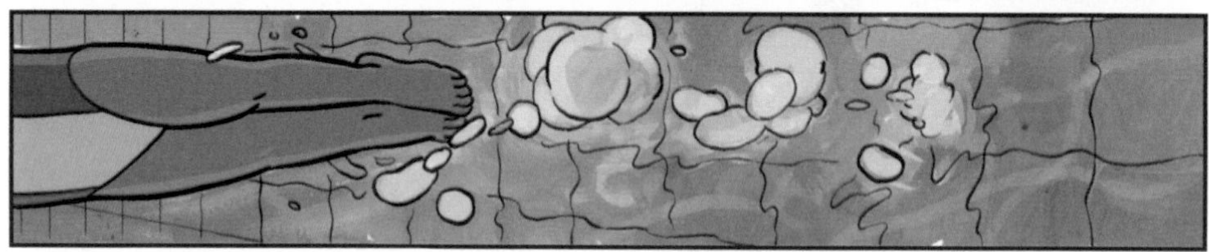

YES!
She did it! She stuck the turn!

She— oh...
Humberto? Are you okay?

Heeeere they come!

Neck and neck, the Manatees close the distance!

Go, Bree!!

Finish strong!

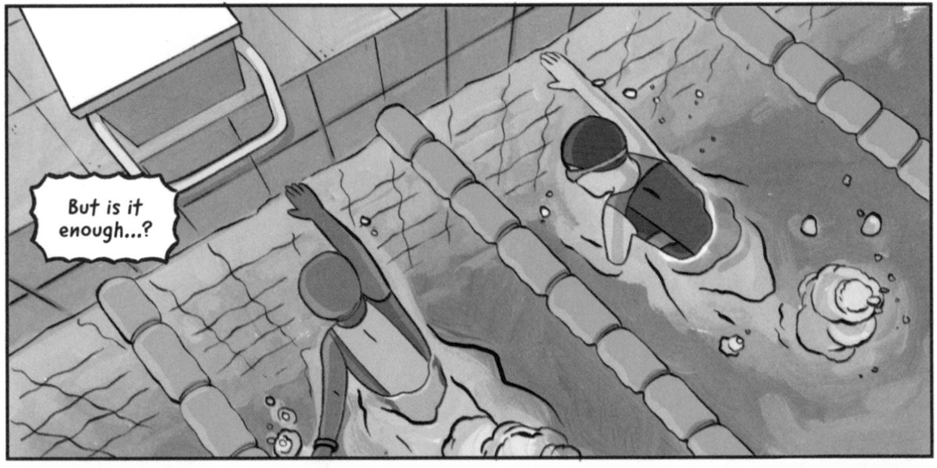
But is it enough...?

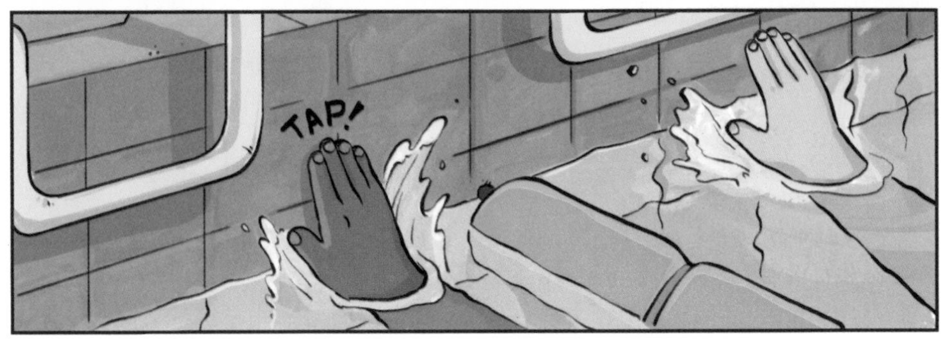
TAP!

YES!!!

YAAAAY!
MANATEES

W-we won!

SWIM SISTERS!

SWIM SISTERS!!!

Whoa! Ha ha!
We did it, Ms. Etta! We won!

And our winner,
Enith Brigitha Middle!

Tinsley?
Keisha... I—

Hmmpph!
flip!

Congrats, you swam a good race.
Thanks Tinsley.

Your coach seems upset...
You **lost**?! With every opportunity we've given you, **this** is how you repay us?!
LOSERS!

We're not losers.
What did you say?

We lost State, but it doesn't make us losers.

Where are you going?

Don't walk away from me!

Finally. What a relief.

Heh heh. Serves her right!

Okay... okay.

We're gonna get ice-cream floats to celebrate. You all wanna come, too?

C'mon! It'll be fun.

Your wall technique is great.
Really? Thanks, Tinsley.

Think you can show me sometime?

Bree!
I passed the math exam!
CONGRATS, Clara!

Thanks, I had a great tutor!

So that's it. You're really going to Holyoke next year?
I'm gonna miss you.

What are you talking about? I still live in the same building as you! You'll see me **EVERY DAY!**
Oh! That's right!

Besides, I'll need tutoring to keep my math scores up.

So long as you help me improve my butterfly.

BET!

Epilogue
Lean back a little, Dad...

Like this?
You're doing great! You'll be swimming soon...
...You're learning fast. Piece by piece, it's all...

...coming together.
The end

Many thanks to:

My uncle Mack for pulling me out of that pool. Meghan Finnegan and Greta Bahn for letting me interview them on competitive swimming and swim coaching (respectively).
Hilary Jenkins for her beautiful color work.
Connie Hernandez, James Lloyd, and Victoria Khrobostova for the background art assists.
My editors Andrew Arnold and Rose Pleuler for their sharp eyes and even sharper minds.
My amazing agent Judy Hansen for her steadfast support and belief in me.
I'd also like to thank David Saylor, Kazu Kibuishi, and Tanis Gibbons.

Further Reading:

Contested Waters: A Social History of Swimming Pools in America by Jeff Wiltse
Undercurrents of Power: Aquatic Culture in the African Diaspora by Kevin Dawson
The Land Was Ours: How Black Beaches Became White Wealth in the Coastal South by Andrew W. Kahrl

HarperAlley is an imprint of HarperCollins Publishers.
Swim Team

For information address HarperCollins Children's Books, a division of HarperCollins Publishers,
195 Broadway, New York, NY 10007.
www.harperalley.com

Library of Congress Control Number: 2021948581
ISBN 978-0-06-305676-3 (pbk.) – ISBN 978-0-06-305677-0 (trade bdg.)
Typography by Chris Dickey and Andrew Arnold

22 23 24 25 26 RTLO 10 9 8 7 6 5 4 3 2 1
First Edition